4/18

D1530979

18

KRYPTO
The SUPERDOG

SUPERMAN CREATED BY
JERRY SIEGEL AND JOE SHUSTER
BY SPECIAL ARRANGEMENT WITH
THE JERRY SIEGEL FAMILY

raintree
a Capstone company — publishers for children

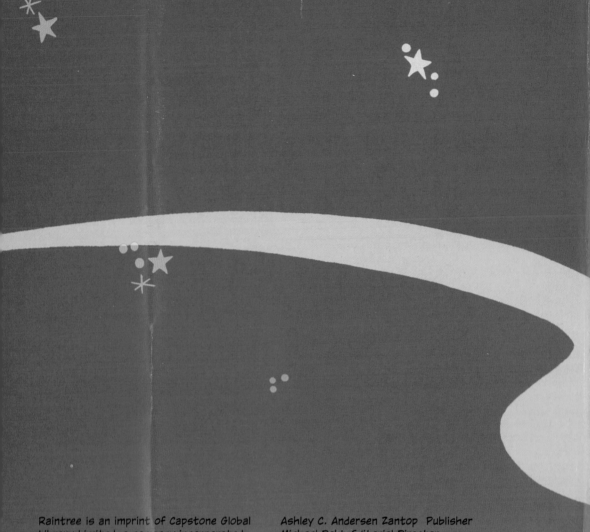

Raintree is an imprint of Capstone Global Library Limited, a company incorporated in England and Wales having its registered office at 7 Pilgrim Street, London, EC4V 6LB – Registered company number: 6695582

First published by Raintree in 2014
The moral rights of the proprietor have been asserted.

Originally published by DC Comics in the US in single magazine form as Krypto The Superdog #5.

Ashley C. Andersen Zantop Publisher
Michael Dahl Editorial Director
Donald Lemke & Sean Tulien Editors
Bob Lentz Art Director
Hilary Wacholz Designer

DC COMICS
Kristy Quinn Original US Editor

ISBN 978 1 406 27954 2

Printed and bound in China.
17 16 15
10 9 8 7 6 5 4 3 2 1

British Library Cataloguing in Publication Data
A full catalogue record for this book is available from the British Library.

KRYPTO
The SUPERDOG™

Three Naughty Doggies!

JESSE LEON MCCANN.................................WRITER
SCOTT COHN ....PENCILLER
AL NICKERSON...INKER
DAVE TANGUAY ....COLOURIST
DAVE TANGUAY ....LETTERER

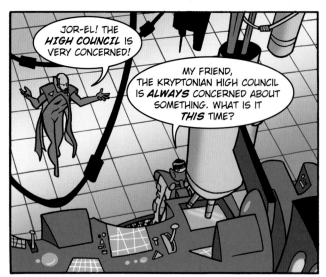

JOR-EL! THE *HIGH COUNCIL* IS VERY CONCERNED!

MY FRIEND, THE *KRYPTONIAN HIGH COUNCIL* IS *ALWAYS* CONCERNED ABOUT SOMETHING. WHAT IS IT *THIS* TIME?

RECENTLY, YOU SENT *GENERAL ZOD* AND HIS *ACCOMPLICES* INTO *EXILE* IN THE *PHANTOM ZONE.*

YES, THEY WERE VICIOUS *CRIMINALS.*

WELL, GENERAL ZOD HAS LEFT US SOME... *PROBLEMS.*

WHAT DO YOU MEAN?

ZOD LEFT US HIS *THREE NAUGHTY DOGGIES.*

WHATEVER SHALL WE DO WITH THEM?

DOM

VILEA

TRONK

GROWL!

SNARL!

SNAP!

"IT DIDN'T TAKE LONG FOR JOR-EL TO COME UP WITH A *SOLUTION*...

THE MATTER IS EASILY SOLVED, MY FRIEND, FOR I SHALL SEND THESE THREE VICIOUS CANINES TO A PLANET THAT ENCIRCLES *SIRIUS, THE DOG STAR.*

SIRIUS?

SSSSSSSSS!

GRRRRRR!

COMPLETELY. THERE THEY SHALL LIVE AMONG THEIR *OWN* KIND.

GRRRRRRR! HOW DARE THE *HAIRLESS ONES* SEND US AWAY!

SHRED!

TEAR!

RIP!

SHVOOOM!

WARNING! WARNING! TAMPERING WITH THE *SHIP'S WIRING* IS NOT ADVISED.

"TOO BAD THE DOGS WRECKED THE ROCKET'S *ANTI-METEOR DEVICE,* BECAUSE A METEOR STRUCK THE SHIP AND THREW THEM FAR *OFF COURSE* ..."

WHAM!

HIBERNATION GAS RELEASED. SLEEP TIGHT!

PSSSSSSS!

WHAT?! NOOOOOO!

"MANY YEARS PASSED, AND THE SHIP LANDED ON EARTH ...

SO THIS IS THE PLANET OF THE DOG STAR? IT'S NOT SO BAD.

YES, VILEA. THE YELLOW RAYS OF THIS PLANET'S SUN MAKE ME FEEL VITAL AND STRONG. IT'S AS IF I COULD ...

...FLY!

WE ALL CAN!

HRRRK!

WHOOOSH!

AND LOOK! WE HAVE REMARKABLE STRENGTH, AS WELL!

EXCELLENT! PERHAPS OUR POWERS ARE GREATER THAN THE INHABITANTS OF THIS PLANET.

ARRRRR!

WHOOSH!

CLUMP

WHOOOSH!

IF SO, WE MAY SUCCEED WHERE GENERAL ZOD FAILED, AND CONQUER AN ENTIRE PLANET! THEN I, DOM, SHALL BE RULER!

"THAT'S WHERE I COME INTO THE STORY. I WAS HAVING A FEAST FIT FOR A KING. MAN! YOU WOULD NOT BELIEVE ALL THE GREAT THINGS TO EAT, JUST LYING AROUND ON THE GROUND AT A TRAVELING CARNIVAL!"

"LITTLE DID I KNOW MY MEAL WAS ABOUT TO BE INTERRUPTED!"

VILEA, TRONK—CREATE SOME *HAVOC*, AND WE'LL SEE WHAT SORT OF *HEROES* THIS PLANET HAS TO CHALLENGE US.

HEEEEY!

HEY, GUYS, I HATE TO BREAK IT TO YOU, BUT *PLAYTIME* IS *OVER*. TIME TO TURN-TAIL AND RUN.

THIS BUMPKIN IS THE *BEST* THEY HAVE TO OFFER?

GRRRRR!

BUMP!

CRASH!

POPCORN

HAVEN'T YOU HEARD OF ME? I'M *SUPERCAT*, THE *CAT OF STEEL*!

NOW, UNLESS YOU WANT ME TO DROP YOU ON YOUR *CABOOSE*, YOU'LL *VAMOOSE*.

WHAT AN *ANNOYING* CREATURE. I'D BE DELIGHTED TO *CRUSH* IT FOR YOU.

HOLD ON, *HEH HEH!* LET'S NOT BE *HASTY!* MAYBE WE SHOULD TALK THIS OVER.

JUST *REMOVE* IT FROM OUR SIGHT, VILEA.

SOMEBODY NEEDS TO TEACH THOSE NAUGHTY DOGGIES SOME MANNERS. SOMEBODY LIKE *SUPERCAT!*

LIGHTS! STREAKY! *ACTION!*

PUH-TUH, PUH-TUH-PUH-TA!

PING! PING! PEW!

MY PLEASURE!

WHOA! WHOA! WHOA! HOLD ON, LADY, THIS AIN'T GOOD FOR MY *DIGESTION!*

WHIR!
WHIR!
WHIR!
WHIR!

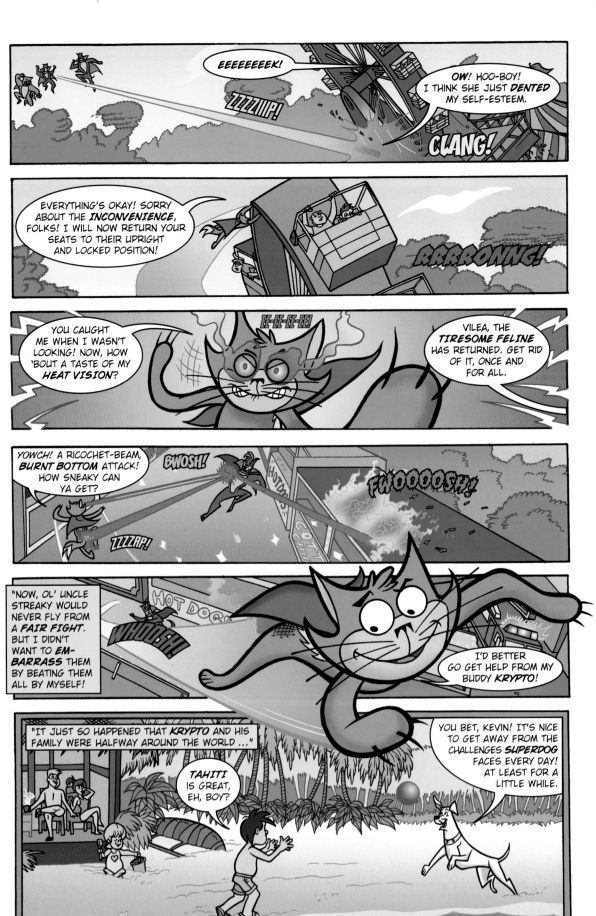

AH!

HIYA, GUYS!

STREAKY? WHAT ARE *YOU* DOING HERE?

COME OVER HERE! I'VE GOT SOMETHING TO SHOW YOU.

WHY? IS THERE *TROUBLE* IN *METROPOLIS?*

UH... NOT ANYMORE.

YOU MIGHT SAY TROUBLE *FOLLOWED* ME *HERE.*

YOU! I REMEMBER YOU!

AND *I* REMEMBER YOU— THE *WHELP* THAT BELONGED TO JOR-EL.

HOW *FORTUNATE.* YOU AND YOUR NEW WORLD WILL *BOW DOWN* TO ME.

WHO *ARE* THEY, BOY?

JUST SOME *BAD DOGS* I THOUGHT I'D NEVER SEE AGAIN.

THIS IS *YOUR* HAIRLESS ONE? PERHAPS AFTER I'VE *DEFEATED* YOU, I'LL MAKE HIM *MY PET.*

KEVIN! RUN BACK TO THE BUNGALOW AND TAKE YOUR FAMILY INSIDE. I HAVE A FEELING THINGS ARE GOING TO GET *ROUGH* OUT HERE!

BECAUSE GETTING RID OF NAUGHTY DOGGIES LOOKS LIKE A JOB...

WHRRRRR!

...FOR **KRYPTO** the SUPERDOG

SPECIAL EFFECTS AND CAPES. HOW *QUAINT.*

THAT'S WHAT I'M TALKIN' 'BOUT!

MY, HOW *HANDSOME* YOU ARE IN YOUR *CLOAK* AND KRYPTONIAN EMBLEM. I *LOVE* A DOG IN UNIFORM.

WELL,...ER,... *GULP*...GEE, *THANKS!*

HERE, *GOOD-LOOKING*, I THINK YOU'LL GET A *KICK* OUT OF THIS!

PUNT!

OOH! THAT'LL LEAVE A *BRUISE!*

OOF!

WHAP! SNAP! WHAP! SNAP! WHAP! SNAP!

YIP! DIDN'T SEE *THAT* COMING!

MOM! *DAD!* WE HAVE TO GET INSIDE! A BIG...*MONSOON* IS COMING THIS WAY!

HA! KWYPTO PLAY WIF *BLACK* DOGGIES. HA HA!

MONSOON? BUT IT'S A *CLEAR*, BEAUTIFUL DAY!

YOU'VE *OVERSTAYED* YOUR WELCOME ON THIS ISLAND. HERE'S SOMETHING TO GET YOU *GOING!*

AHHHHH!

FWSSSSSSSH!

CLONK!

IT *BLOWS* YOUR MIND, DOESN'T IT?

FWSSSSSSSH!

UH... M-MAYBE YOU'RE *RIGHT*, SON. LET GET UNDERCOVER!

OH, *DEAR!* WHERE'S KRYPTO?

HE'LL BE ALL RIGHT... I *HOPE.*

ARGHH! WHA-WHATS HAPPENING TO US?

IT'S CALLED *KRYPTONITE*, AND YOU PUPPIES HAVE BEEN *PUNK'D*!

I BORROWED IT FROM SUPERMAN'S *FORTRESS OF SOLITUDE*.

ROH!

I FEEL SO *WEAK*!

THIS *LEAD-LINED MAT* WILL PROTECT US FROM THE KRYPTONITE INSIDE. COME ON, STREAKY, LET'S FIND THE *ROCKET* THESE THREE CAME IN. *RUFF, RUFF AND AWAY!*

HURRY BACK, BOY!

MOAN!

"BACK IN METROPOLIS, IT DIDN'T TAKE US LONG TO FIND THE *ROCKET*...

HEY! WHY DON'T WE BURY THIS IN *MY* BACKYARD, SO I COULD HAVE A *ROCKET PLAYHOUSE* TOO?

NO, WE *NEED* THE ROCKET TO SEND THESE VILLAINS *AWAY*.

BUT TO *WHERE*? MAYBE THERE'S A *CLUE* ON THE INSIDE.

GREETINGS! THIS SHIP WAS MEANT TO LAND NEAR SIRIUS, THE DOG STAR. UNFORTUNATELY, IT LANDED ON EARTH, INSTEAD.

I WILL NOW *INSTRUCT YOU* ON HOW TO *REPROGRAM* THE SHIP'S ONBOARD COMPUTER.

HOLY MACARONI!! NICE TV PICTURE!

IT'S A *HOLOGRAM RECORDING*, STREAKY.

"SUPERDOG *RESET* THE ROCKET'S CONTROLS, AND THAT WAS THE *LAST* WE SAW OF THE THREE NAUGHTY DOGGIES.

SHVOOOM!

MANY YEARS FROM NOW, THEY'LL LAND ON A PLANET IN THE *SIRIUS SYSTEM*, WHERE EVERYONE HAS TO ACT *SERIOUS* ALL THE TIME AND THEY NEVER HAVE ANY FUN. THE END!

"SIRIUS" ISN'T SPELT THE SAME AS "SERIOUS." YOU *MADE THAT UP*, UNCLE STREAKY!

TELL US ANOTHER STORY! PLEASE!

PLEASE! PLEASE! PLEASE!

"SIGH!" THE *PRICE* OF BEING A SUPERHERO IS HIGH. BUT *SOMEBODY'S* GOT TO DO IT!

The END

AH! CONNECTICUT IN THE FALL...

BEAUTIFUL LAKES, BLUE SKY, LEAVES OF A THOUSAND COLORS, AND...

...BATS!

SHOO! GET AWAY!

SKREEE! SKREE!

THAT'S NOT BATS!

JESSE LEON MCCANN — WRITER
MIN S. KU — PENCILLER
JEFF ALBRECHT — INKER
DAVE TANGUAY — LETTERER/COLORIST
RACHEL GLUCKSTERN—ASST. EDITOR
JOAN HILTY— EDITOR

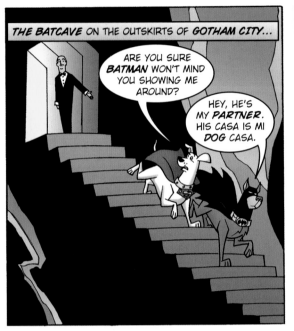

THE BATCAVE ON THE OUTSKIRTS OF GOTHAM CITY...

ARE YOU SURE BATMAN WON'T MIND YOU SHOWING ME AROUND?

HEY, HE'S MY PARTNER. HIS CASA IS MI DOG CASA.

...SUDDENLY, THERE WERE A THOUSAND BATS ALL AROUND ME!

THEY TOOK MY GRANDPA'S *GOLD* POCKET WATCH AND MADE ME LOSE MY *FAVORITE* FISHING POLE!

ANYONE *ELSE* HAVE A RUN-IN WITH THESE THIEVING BATS?

"YES, THERE WERE A NUMBER OF INCIDENTS...

SKREEE!

HEY!

"...THEY SWARMED THROUGH TOWN, STEALING *EVERYTHING* IN THEIR PATH.

"THEY ROBBED THE BANK, AND MADE OFF WITH SEVERAL THOUSAND *DOLLARS*.

SKREEE!

"THE JEWELRY STORE OWNER BLEW A *GASKET* AND ENDED UP IN THE *HOSPITAL*."

SKREEE!

SKREEE!

ALL RIGHT, JIM. *I'LL* LOOK INTO IT.

THANKS, BATMAN. I'D STICK AROUND AND HELP, BUT I'M DUE BACK IN GOTHAM CITY.

END TRANSMISSION.

HMM... JIM GORDON JUST *HAPPENS* TO BE IN A TOWN WHEN THERE'S A *BAT* ATTACK. *COINCIDENCE*? OR IS SOMEONE JUST TRYING TO GET MY *ATTENTION*?

I NEED YOUR *HELP* ON THIS ONE, BOYS.

LATER THAT NIGHT...

TELL ME *WHY* WE'RE DOING THIS AGAIN, LOU?

I KNOW OUR MISSION IS TO KEEP BATMAN *BUSY*, BUT IF WE CAN *KEEP SOME LOOT*, TOO, IT'S JUST ICING ON THE *CAKE*. HA HA HA HA!

I *LIKE* CAKE, LOU! HA HA HA!

SKREEE!

SKREEE!

KEEP LAUGHING, LOWLIFES. YOUR *CHUCKLES* ARE ABOUT TO MEET MY *KNUCKLES*.

AY YI YI! IT'S BATMAN!

SWIING!

HEY, BUD! WATCH WHERE YOU'RE GOIN'!

I TOLD YOU THE *BLINDERS* WERE A BAD IDEA, LOU!

SWERVE!

WHAT ARE YOU DOIN', BUD?!

I'M RIDIN' WITH YOU, LOU!

THEN WHO'S *DRIVIN'*?

AIIIEEEEEE!

IMPRESSIVE... IN A *DIMWITTED HYENA* SORT OF WAY.

CRASH!

I CAN'T BELIEVE IT! THE BATS HAVE *DISAPPEARED* AGAIN.

RUN, BUD, RUN!

SHOULD I *ROUND UP* BUD AND LOU FOR QUESTIONING?

NOT YET. WE NEED TO KEEP UP THE *BATMAN RUSE* A BIT LONGER.

BESIDES, I THINK I'VE *DISCOVERED* SOMETHING... INTERESTING.

SOON...

HEY, *LOOK*, BUD! OUR BATS HAVE BEEN *WORKING OVERTIME* AND LEFT US A *PRESENT!*

THAT'S GREAT, LOU! NOW WE CAN BUY *ALL THE CAKE* WE WANT.

WE'RE *TRAPPED*, LOU! OUR CAKES ARE *COOKED!*

SPROING!

COOL IT WITH THE *CAKE THING*, BUD.

TIME FOR US TO HAVE A LONG OVERDUE *CHAT*, BOYS.

I DON'T CARE IF IT TAKES *ALL NIGHT*, YOU'RE GOING TO GIVE ME SOME ANSWERS.

OH NO! *ALL NIGHT?* DID YOU HEAR THAT, LOU?

LOUD AND *CLEAR*, BUD. AND I'M SENDING *THE BOSS* THE MESSAGE.

HA HA HA HA HA!

THAT'S GREAT! WE'VE GOT YOU *JUST WHERE* WE WANT YOU, BATMAN!

THERE'S ONLY *ONE* PROBLEM...

BATMAN IS MY PARTNER. I'M *BAT-HOUND!*

TEE-HEE-HEE-HEE! MOOOO!

GASP!

I GOTTA *TEXT* THE BOSS! BATMAN IS ON TO HIM!

I DON'T *THINK* SO! I'LL TAKE THAT.

FINE! OUR BATS WILL *STEAL* ME ANOTHER ONE. *HAW!*

I HATE TO BREAK IT TO YOU, BUT WE *FOUND* YOUR BATS, HIDING RIGHT HERE IN *PLAIN SIGHT*.

YOU COULD MAKE THEM DO YOUR BIDDING BECAUSE THEY'RE *NOT* BATS AT ALL, THEY'RE *ROBOTS*.

SOON TO BE *DEACTIVATED* ROBOTS. LOOKS LIKE THE *JOKER'S PLANS* ARE JUST ABOUT WASHED UP!

Superdog Jokes!

**WHAT KIND OF DOG SPECIALIZES
IN PRIZE FIGHTS?**

A BOXER!

WHAT DO YOU CALL A CUTE RETRIEVER?

LABRADOR-ABLE!

**WHAT HAPPENS WHEN KRYPTO
FIGHTS SNOOKY WOOKUMS?**

FUR FLIES!

**WHAT DOES A KITTEN
CALL A REALLY BAD DAY?**

A CAT-TASTROPHE!

Creators

JESSE LEON MCCANN WRITER

Jesse Leon McCann is a *New York Times* Top-Ten Children's Book Writer, as well as a prolific all-ages comics writer. His credits include Pinky and the Brain, Animaniacs, and Looney Tunes for DC Comics; Scooby-Doo and Shrek 2 for Scholastic; and The Simpsons and Futurama for Bongo Comics. He lives in Los Angeles with his wife and four cats.

SCOTT COHN PENCILLER

Scott Cohn is an experienced illustrator who has worked with clients such as DC Comics, WWE, Harper Collins, Mirage, Dynamite, MTV, HBO, A&E, and Time Inc., just to name a few.

AL NICKERSON INKER

Al Nickerson has done illustration work for DC Comics, Archie, and Marvel.

DAVE TANGUAY COLOURIST/LETTERER

David Tanguay has over 20 years of experience in the comic book industry. He has worked as an editor, layout artist, colourist, and letterer. He has also done web design, and he taught computer graphics at the State University of New York.

Glossary

ACCOMPLICE someone who helps another person commit a crime

CONQUER to defeat and take control of an enemy

DEACTIVATED turned off or disabled

EXILE to send someone away from their home

HASTY too quick or hurried

HAVOC great damage and chaos

INHABITANTS people or animals that live in a certain place

MONSOON very strong wind that blows from the ocean to the land and brings heavy rains

SUSPECTS individuals thought to be guilty of a crime

Visual Questions & Prompts

1. BASED ON WHAT YOU KNOW FROM THIS STORY, WHY IS IT IMPORTANT FOR KRYPTO AND ACE TO MAKE EVERYONE THINK THAT BATMAN IS THE ONE WHO HELPED THEM?

2. IN THIS PANEL, THE MAN IN PURPLE IS REFERRING TO THE STAR, SIRIUS, BUT IT'S ALSO A PLAY ON WORDS, OR A PUN. WHAT IS THE SECOND MEANING OF HIS RESPONSE?

3. IF YOU COULD CREATE A PACK OF ROBOTIC ANIMALS, WHAT KIND WOULD YOU MAKE AND WHAT WOULD YOU DO WITH THEM?

4. BETWEEN THESE PANELS, WHY DO YOU THINK THE CREATORS MADE A PANEL BORDER WITH THE BATS? HOW DOES IT AFFECT THE WAY YOU READ IT? HOW DOES IT MAKE YOU FEEL?

READ THEM ALL!

NEVER FEAR! *SUPERDOG* IS HERE!